# 58
Cho
7/20/95

# IMANI
## IN THE BELLY

WRITTEN BY DEBORAH M. NEWTON CHOCOLATE

PICTURES BY ALEX BOIES

BridgeWater Books

Text copyright © 1994 by Deborah M. Newton Chocolate.
Illustrations copyright © 1994 by Alex Boies.
Designed by Leslie Bauman.
Published by BridgeWater Books, an imprint of Troll
Associates, Inc.
Printed in the United States of America.
10  9  8  7  6  5  4  3  2  1

Library of Congress Cataloging-in-Publication Data
Chocolate, Deborah M. Newton.
    Imani in the belly / by Deborah M. Newton
Chocolate; pictures by Alex Boies.
        p.    cm.
    Summary: Imani's faith helps her save herself and
her children from the belly of the King of Beasts.
    ISBN 0-8167-3466-6 (lib. bdg.)—
ISBN 0-8167-3467-4 (pbk.)
    [1. Folklore—Africa.    2. Animals—Folklore.]
I. Boies, Alex, ill.    II. Title.
PZ8.1.C4517Im    1994
398.21—dc20    [E]    93-33803

To my sister, Alma Louise Newton Smith—
Thanks be to our mother, whose faith has freed us all.
With love,
DMC

This is dedicated to my mother, Gaby McIver.
With love,
Al

A long time ago in a small village in Africa lived a woman named Imani, which means "faith." Imani and her three children lived a full day's journey from the city and the marketplace. So each year at harvest time, Imani had to travel a full day to sell her crops of cassavas, sugar cane, and yams. Whenever she was away, Imani left her children to look after one another.

Each day herds of wild animals thundered past Imani's village. The people cried out, "Run for your lives!" And, at the sound of their neighbors' voices, other villagers threw down their digging sticks and scattered back to their huts. With their children and farm animals, they hid behind kraal fences, trembling and crying with fear.

And each day, when the dust settled over the land, there were fewer and fewer people left, for the King of Beasts was swallowing up the villagers, their children, and their animals.

One morning, as Imani prepared to leave for the
marketplace, she told her children, "My little *watoto*,
as soon as I leave the village you must hurry inside the
hut. When you hear the wild animals approaching, you
must hide from the stampeding herd."

"Yes, *mama mzazi*," cried the children obediently.
But as soon as Imani had gone, they wandered off to a
rain pond near the forest, far from the village.

So far away had the children wandered that they did
not hear the cry, "Run for your lives!" as chattering
hyenas, screeching monkeys, and trumpeting
elephants raced past the village to the very forest
where they played.

Imani's eldest child was the first to see the animals coming toward them. Leading the way was Simba, the horrible King of Beasts with a roar of rolling thunder. His giant strides made the jungle floor tremble.

Quickly, the children hid behind a towering grove of doum palms, but the hungry beast soon encircled them.

In a voice that made palm trees stop whispering in the wind, the beast said, "Come closer, my little ones! I can hardly see you."

And as the children moved closer, Simba rolled out his tongue and swallowed them up.

When Imani returned from the marketplace, a frightened neighbor greeted her. "Imani," began the woman breathlessly, "while you were away Simba swallowed up your three children."

Imani was so stricken with grief, she cried herself to sleep. While she slept, her own *mama mzazi* came to her in a dream.

"My *watoto*," Imani's mother tried to comfort her. "Why are you crying so?"

"Mama," explained Imani, "a terrible beast has swallowed my children."

"Then you must gather your faith and go after the beast," Imani's mother advised her. "Go now, and gather some meat and some dry sticks, and sharpen two stones. When you have done this, you must go in search of your children and the beast."

"What should I do when I see the beast?" she asked.

"Let your faith guide you," answered her mother. And then she was gone.

When Imani awoke, she gathered meat and dry sticks, and sharpened two stones as her mother had instructed. Then she set out along the path in search of her children and the beast.

She climbed rolling hills and barren mountains. Through the blazing heat of daylight, Imani wandered across the jungle, until she could travel no more. At last, she slept beneath the full moon of the night.

At sunrise, she began her journey again. Imani had not gone far when she fell upon her knees.

"*Mama, weeeeeeeee!*" she cried.

Before her was a herd of wild animals, grazing along a kraal fence by the edge of a river. Among them was Simba, King of Beasts.

Trembling with fear, Imani crept closer and closer until she was standing in Simba's great, dark, terrible shadow. Surrounded by a circle of hungry wild animals, Imani began to plead, "Please, sir! Please, tell me what you have done with my children!"

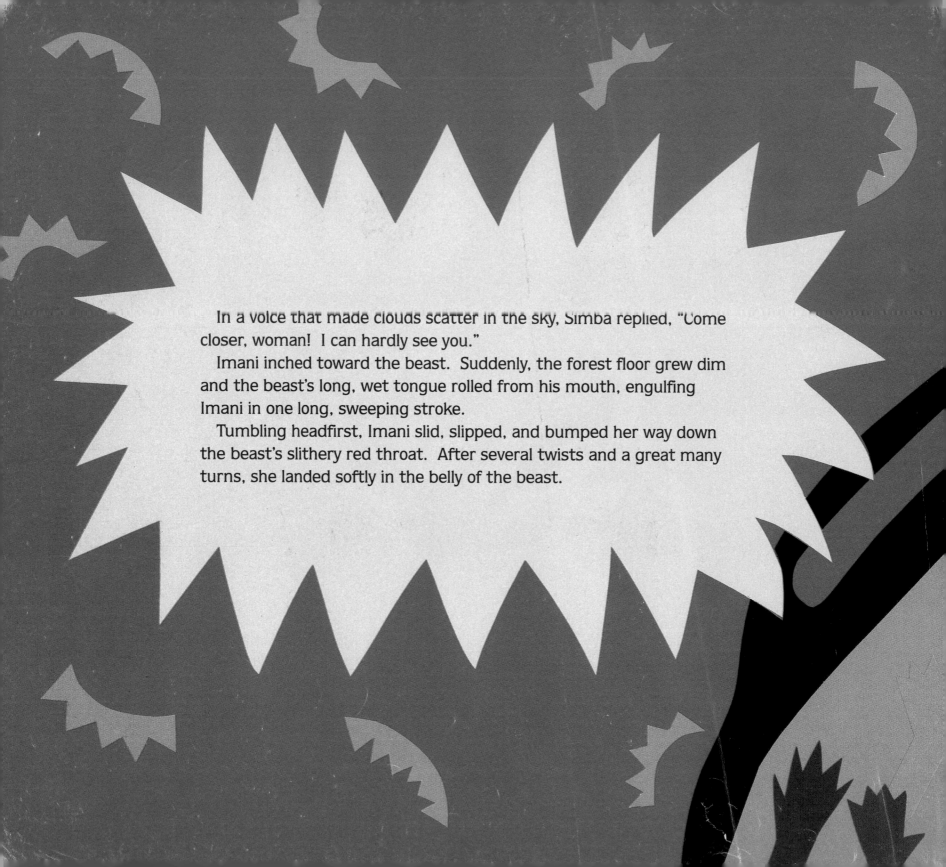

In a voice that made clouds scatter in the sky, Simba replied, "Come closer, woman!  I can hardly see you."

Imani inched toward the beast.  Suddenly, the forest floor grew dim and the beast's long, wet tongue rolled from his mouth, engulfing Imani in one long, sweeping stroke.

Tumbling headfirst, Imani slid, slipped, and bumped her way down the beast's slithery red throat.  After several twists and a great many turns, she landed softly in the belly of the beast.

When Simba opened his mouth to let out a satisfied "Ggggroar!"
sunlight shone down on Imani's three children and all of the villagers
and their animals.

"Imani!" exclaimed her friends and neighbors. "You have found us."

"Mama," cried her children. "We are so frightened here, and we have
nothing to fill our bellies."

Quickly, Imani knelt down, struck her stones of flint together, and
blew softly on the wooden sticks to build a fire. Then she cooked the
meat from her bag for her children and the villagers to eat.

But the heat from the fire stung the beast's belly, and he let out a full-throated "Arghhhh!" Not only did his belly ache, but his throat was parched from the rising smoke of the fire. Simba called the other animals together to ask them what he should do.

Imani pressed her ear to the wall of the beast's belly and listened as chattering hyenas, screeching monkeys, and trumpeting elephants all offered their advice.

"You must eat *eto* from the calabash bowl, O Great One!" said Monkey nervously.

"No! No!" offered Hyena, chattering wildly. "You must stick your head in the honeybee hive like this, Great Simba."

*Buzzzzzzzzzzzzzzzzzzzzzzzzzzzzzzzzzz!*

"Not that!" screamed Elephant. "The bees will sting Simba's head one thousand times."

"That is true," laughed Hyena. "But at least it will take his mind off his stomachache."

All the while, the beast moaned and roared and rolled in the mud. At last, he stuck his head in the kraal fence and lay there, wisps of white smoke floating out of his nose.

In the distance Monkey saw a crowd of shouting villagers armed with sticks and stones heading for Simba. Monkey took one look at the angry villagers and said to the animals, "You must hurry! Those of you who herd in the grasslands must go to the grasslands. Those of you who gather in the bush must flee to that place. As for me and my cousins, we will run away to the trees."

Quickly, all the wild animals ran away. Hyena raced to the grasslands. Bird flew to the bush. And Elephant and Giraffe galloped to the plains.

All this time, Imani had been planning her own escape. With hemp rope from the necks of goats and cows, she formed a long chain. "My brothers and sisters, we must help one another if we are to escape," she told the villagers. Then, linking themselves together, they began the long, hard climb up the slithery throat of the beast.

But Imani soon discovered that climbing up was twice as hard as sliding down. For every three steps she made, Imani slid back one. So the villagers began to sing out, "Faith be to Imani! Faith be to Imani!" to encourage her on her way. Imani began to climb higher and higher, until she reached the beast's mouth. She tied the rope to the beast's red-hot, swollen tonsils and began to pull the other villagers up, one by one.

When they had all reached the beast's mouth, Simba let out a cough that sent everyone flying onto the jungle floor.

All of the people looked up at the sky, for it had been awhile since they had seen sunset. The oxen sniffed at the wind, trying to pick up the scent of wild animals. But all of the animals had scattered to the places where they can still be found to this day.

After the fire in his belly went out, Simba ran away from the plains and has never been seen or heard from again.

As for the villagers who had faith in Imani, they all joined hands with her. And because they believed in themselves and their power, the people became a great nation.

**"THANKS BE TO IMANI, WHOSE FAITH HAS FREED US ALL!"**

Inspiration for *Imani in the Belly* came from a collection of folktales gathered by G. M. Theal in his 1886 book, *Kaffir Folk-Lore*. The name of the character of Imani (ee MAH nee) is from the East African language of Swahili. *Imani* means "faith."